a very CRANKY book

That's me.

a very
CRANKY
book

Nope. Not today.

X F
DITER

KIOSK

OSHAWA PUBLIC LIBRARIES
39364902618664
pr07100549

DiTerlizzi, Angela
A very cranky book

Nov. 30, 2023

ANGELA & TONY DiTERLIZZI

Quill Tree Books
An Imprint of HarperCollins Publishers

You should go find something else to do—
Ride a bike, play a game, draw a picture . . .

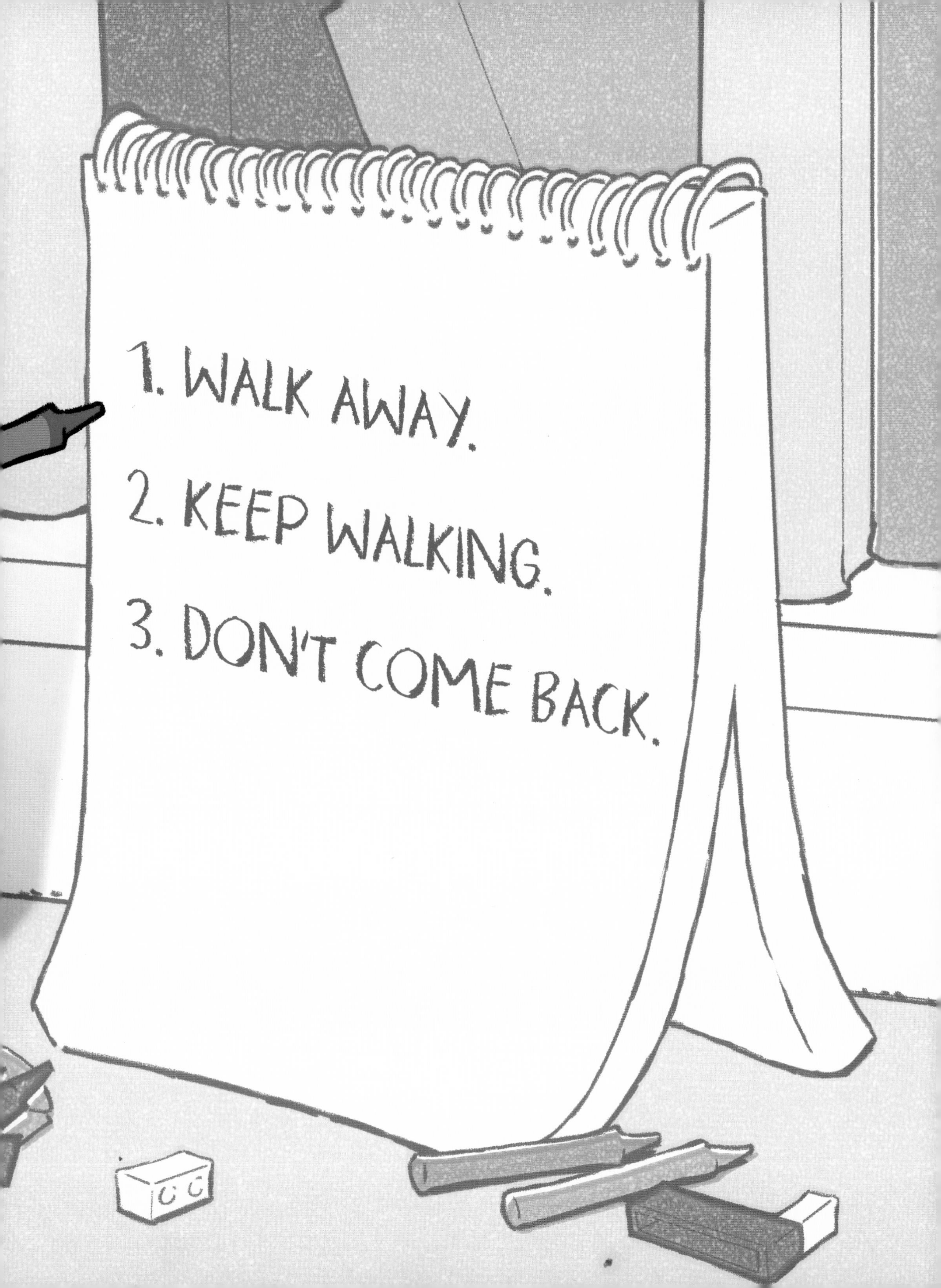
1. WALK AWAY.
2. KEEP WALKING.
3. DON'T COME BACK.

Gather round, friends.
Story time is about to begin!

We've been through so much, pal–
the good times, the bad times . . . the
cranky times.
Thanks for sticking by me.
Now let's get reading!

THE END

For our cranky friend, Chrissy
–Ang & T

Quill Tree Books is an imprint of HarperCollins Publishers.

A Very Cranky Book
Copyright © 2023 by Angela DiTerlizzi and Tony DiTerlizzi
All rights reserved. Printed in the United States of America.
No part of this book may be used or reproduced in any manner whatsoever without written permission
except in the case of brief quotations embodied in critical articles and reviews. For information address
HarperCollins Children's Books, a division of HarperCollins Publishers, 195 Broadway, New York, NY 10007.
www.harpercollinschildrens.com
Library of Congress Control Number: 2022004675
ISBN 978-0-06-320667-0

The artist used an actual (possibly cranky) book and
Photoshop magic to create the digital illustrations for this book.
23 24 25 PC 10 9 8 7 6 5 4 3 2
First Edition

Zzz. . .